MY COUSIN THE
# MINOTAUR

**ReadZone Books Limited**

www.ReadZoneBooks.com

© in this edition 2017 ReadZone Books Limited

This print edition published in cooperation with Fiction Express, who first published this title in weekly instalments as an interactive e-book.

**FICTION EXPRESS**

Fiction Express
Boolino Limited
First Floor Office, 2 College Street,
Ludlow, Shropshire SY8 1AN
www.fictionexpress.co.uk

Find out more about Fiction Express on pages 55–56.

Design: Laura Harrison & Keith Williams
Cover Images: Bigstock

© in the text 2016 Saviour Pirotta
The moral right of the author has been asserted.

ISBN 978-1-78322-603-0

Printed in Malta by Melita Press

# MY COUSIN THE
# MINOTAUR

by Saviour Pirotta

**What do other readers think?**

Here are some comments left on the Fiction Express blog about this book:

*"The story was very good."*
**Dacre, Isle of Man**

*"You have done a good job. I love minotaurs"*
**Nico S, Telford**

*"I loved it because it was fantabulous. I could imagine it all."*
**Charlie, Cannock**

*"We really liked your story."*
**Year 2, Willow, Meadowside Primary School, Gloucester**

*"I love your story."*
**Olivia, Isle of Man**

*"I love that it links with our topic myths and legends."*
**Cameron, Telford**

*"It was amazing. You rock with stories : )"*
**Luke L, Isle of Man**

# Contents

# Chapter 1

# A Mystery

Princess Chloe was very excited. She had been invited to stay with her cousin Prince Alexander on the island of Axos. The island was famous for its mysterious caves and mountains. They were going to have lots of fun together.

Chloe put on her favourite tunic and headed down to the great hall for dinner. She was looking forward to meeting her cousin for the first time. She stared wide-eyed at the paintings on the walls along the way. There were beautiful underwater scenes of fish and dolphins.

In the great hall, the king and queen – Chloe's aunt and uncle – were waiting to meet her.

"Good evening," they greeted one another politely.

Chloe bent and kissed them both on the hand.

"Where is Alexander?" she asked, looking around the room.

"He's gone to Athens," said the king.

"He's visiting a sick friend," said the queen at the same time.

Chloe looked from one to the other. *How odd*, she thought. *Neither of them seemed to know where the prince had gone. Alexander had written to say he was looking forward to meeting her. Why would he suddenly decide to go away?*

\* \* \*

As Chloe made her way back to her room after dinner, she heard a muffled roar coming from somewhere below. Something very strange was going on in the palace. She had to find out what it was.

Taking a lamp from the wall, she tiptoed back down the corridor. She made her way past the great hall. The roaring seemed to get louder. There was no one about.

Chloe explored all the rooms on the ground floor. The roaring had stopped, but now she could hear a loud grunting.

*Where was it coming from?*

Looking around the kitchen, Chloe noticed a little door. It was half hidden behind a pile of empty baskets. She pulled it open. Before her lay a long flight of steps, snaking down into darkness.

Carefully, Chloe picked her way down the stairs. They led to a dungeon. And there, snarling at her through the bars, was a hideous monster.

# Chapter 2

# The Minotaur

The monster was half bull, half man – a minotaur!

Chloe fled back up the steps.

"What are you doing here?" said a voice. Standing in the kitchen was a small boy in scruffy clothes.

"I was l-looking for Al-Alexander," stuttered Chloe.

"Well you just found him," said

the boy. "You're Princess Chloe aren't you?"

Chloe nodded.

"I'm Tiro, one of the servants. I heard your aunt and uncle lying to you earlier," the boy said. "The prince is not in Athens or with a sick friend. He's… he's under a curse."

"A curse?" gasped Chloe.

"Yes," sighed Tiro, wiping a tear from his eye. "That monster is really Alexander – your cousin and my friend. The gods turned him into a minotaur because the king offered them rotten fruit at the harvest festival."

"But that's unfair," replied Chloe. "My uncle should be punished for this insult, not Alexander."

"That's the way of the gods," sniffed the boy.

Chloe raised the lamp. "Is there any way to save him?"

Tiro nodded eagerly. "Yes, there's a magic flower with powerful nectar inside. If Alexander drank just one drop of that nectar, he would become a boy again.... Trouble is the flower only grows on

Mount Olympus, the home of the gods. I've no way to get there."

Chloe smiled for the first time since she had arrived in Axos. "I have my horse, Nebulus!" she cried. "Hurry, we must get some of this nectar at once."

"B-but I'm a servant," gasped Tiro "I can't just leave the palace… and besides, it's dangerous to travel at night!"

# Chapter 3

# A Setback

Princess Chloe frowned at the servant boy in front of her.

"I'll go alone, then," she declared. "I'd rather DIE than leave my cousin in that state."

She started for the door. "I want to go with you," groaned Tiro, "but… I'll lose my job if I'm not here to light the ovens at dawn."

"Well," said Chloe. "How about if I COMMAND you to come with me? I am a princess and you cannot refuse me. I'll speak up for you when we get back. You won't lose your job."

Tiro grinned. "Very well, then! Let's go, your highness."

They hurried out of the palace towards the stables. Chloe's horse, Nebulus, heard them coming and whinnied softly.

"Shhh," said Chloe. "It's only me, Neb." She got on the horse while Tiro opened the stable gate.

A moment later they were galloping away from the palace.

"Where are we going, your highness?" Tiro asked.

"To the harbour," replied Chloe. "We must find a ship that will take us to the mainland. Then we can ride to Mount Olympus.

* * *

There were four ships in the harbour. One of them was getting ready to sail at dawn. Chloe left Tiro in charge of Neb and marched up the gangplank. She asked to speak to the captain. He nodded grimly as she spoke. "I am sorry," he said. "I can't take any passengers with me."

Chloe held up her head. "I am a princess. I COMMAND you to take us."

The captain shook his head. "I'm sorry, your highness. Orders of the king himself."

"Why would the king stop anyone from leaving the island?" Chloe asked Tiro back on the quay.

"Perhaps to stop news of the minotaur getting out," said Tiro.

"What do we do now?"

"Hmm," said Chloe. "I know what my father would do in a situation like this. He'd consult the oracle."

"You mean one of those mad old women who give advice?"

"Yes," said Chloe. "Is there one on Axos?"

Tiro nodded.

"Then we must go and find her." Chloe announced.

# Chapter 4

# Strange Advice

Half an hour later the two of them were knocking on the door of a small temple. A light came on inside. "Who dares to wake the oracle at this time of night?" asked a shrill voice.

"We need urgent advice," called Tiro.

An old woman came to the door. She was as thin as a rake, with a face like a wrinkled plum.

"How will you pay me?" she croaked.

Chloe took a gold ring from her finger and handed it over. "We need to get off the island as quickly as possible. But we have no ship, only a horse. Can you help us?"

"Only a horse, eh?" cackled the oracle, grabbing the ring. "Only a horse and no ship!"

Suddenly she cocked her head to one side. "Someone is coming after you. Soldiers! Quick, come with me… and bring the horse."

Chloe and Tiro hurried after her to an orchard at the back of the temple. The oracle pointed to an ancient tree in the middle of it. "That is a magic oak, blessed by the gods. Let your horse strike the roots three times with his hoof."

Chloe could hear the soldiers' horses quite clearly now. The oracle started chanting a spell. Chloe nudged Neb closer to the tree. He seemed to understand what she wanted from him. He stepped forward and struck the roots three times.

Suddenly there was a flash of lightning... and a moment later Neb had grown huge wings! They swished and swooshed as he flapped them.

"Quick now, on you get!" cried the old woman.

# Chapter 5

# The Storm

Chloe clambered on to Neb and Tiro followed.

"Hold on tight," warned Chloe. She grabbed the reins and Neb leapt up into the air, his wings flapping gently.

"The gods go with you," shrieked the oracle as the king's soldiers burst into the orchard. Behind the temple, the sun was rising.

"Look," said Tiro. "There's a ship sailing into the harbour."

Chloe frowned. The ship had a square sail with black and white stripes. "It's Prince Theseus!" she gasped. "He must have come to kill the minotaur!"

She tugged on the reins to make Neb fly faster.

"That's not all," groaned Tiro. "There's a storm brewing. I can smell it in the air."

"A storm?" Chloe looked around her, puzzled. "But the sky is perfectly clear."

Tiro was right, though. The air turned suddenly cold. Huge, dark clouds appeared from nowhere. Rain started lashing down.

"The wind is blowing us back towards Axos," Tiro shouted. "The gods are trying to stop us reaching Mount Olympus."

Chloe forced herself to stay calm so she could think. Something her tutor had once said niggled at her mind. What was it? Ah – yes!

*Storm clouds always hang LOW in the sky.*

Chloe knew what she had to do.

She leaned forward and whispered in Neb's ear.

Suddenly, the horse swooped upwards. They rose through the storm into the clear sky above. Up here there was no rain or wind, just dazzling sunshine. And silence!

## *Chapter 6*

# The Home of the Gods

By late afternoon Neb was flying over the mainland. Now Mount Olympus loomed high above them. Chloe could see lights twinkling in the gods' palaces. The sound of harp music drifted on the air.

And then, right out of the blue, a thunderbolt exploded above their heads. It sent Neb reeling and

Chloe found herself hurtling towards the ground. She could hear Tiro screaming in her ear as she fell. Any moment now, they would smash against the rocks.

Chloe closed her eyes and prayed to her favourite goddess.

"Please, don't let me die."

THUD!

Chloe landed on something soft – something that got in her nose and made her sneeze. She had fallen straight on to a haystack. Tiro landed right beside her. They rolled to the ground, gasping for breath.

"My, you are lucky," chuckled a booming voice nearby.

Chloe opened her eyes to see a hideous giant standing above her. His eyes were blood red and his arms were covered in scars. He held a huge hammer in his hands.

Tiro sat up. "You are the gods' blacksmith. My father told me all about you."

"I'm a god too," sniffed the giant. "But the others won't let me live on Mount Olympus. They think I am too ugly. I live in an underground cave instead."

"That's not fair," said Chloe. "It's not what you look like on the outside that makes you beautiful or ugly. It's what's in your heart."

"Bless you," said the giant. "I wish that snooty lot up there would think the same. I saw them shooting that thunderbolt at you. That's why I moved the haystack so you would land on it."

"Thank you," said Chloe.

"Your horse is safe by the way, although I think his left wing is injured. He's grazing in the valley just over there. Now what are you doing here at the home of the gods?"

Chloe and Tiro told him their story.

"The nectar is easy to get once you're at the top of Mount Olympus," said the giant. "But getting there is another matter. The gods guard the mountain passes. Luckily, I know of a secret passage inside the mountain. It's the safest way to get to the top. You have been kind to me so come, I'll show you the entrance...."

# Chapter 7

# Dogs!

The giant led Chloe and Tiro to
a cave.

"The secret passage starts here," he
said, handing Chloe a burning torch.

"Where we will find the nectar?"
asked Tiro.

"Nectar is the juice of a magic
yellow flower," said the giant.
"You'll find it in the Garden of

Heavenly Scents behind the big temple. Good luck! And beware of the centaurs. They guard all the temples."

He stomped away, leaving Chloe and Tiro to enter the cave alone. They stepped inside. Its sandy floor was littered with rusted swords and old wine flasks.

A sudden growl made Chloe start in terror. Three pairs of red eyes were glaring at her in the darkness!

"They're…they're only dogs," stammered Tiro. "G-get back. Good boys."

The three dogs tried to leap forward, only to be pulled back by something. Chloe heard the clink of metal. The dogs were chained to the wall, blocking the secret passageway. Chloe moved a bit closer with the torch – and gasped. The three dogs were actually one massive creature. It had three heads, each full of razor-sharp teeth!

"How are we going to get past it?" wondered Tiro. "Those weapons and flasks on the ground must have been dropped by people running away from the dog."

Chloe picked up a wine flask.

"Yuck!" Tiro held his nose as she pulled out the stopper, "the wine's turned to vinegar."

"That's what I was hoping for," said Chloe. She splashed the smelly liquid all over herself and handed the flask to Tiro. "You do the same. Then follow me."

Tiro did as Chloe asked. The two of them crept further inside the cave. Their hearts were pounding. The dog's three noses sniffed, then it shrank back against the wall, whining loudly.

Chloe darted past it, pulling Tiro behind her. "Our gardener back home sprinkles vinegar round his vegetables," she explained as they hurried on. "It stops the palace dogs from trampling all over them. Dogs *hate* the smell of vinegar."

"So do I," grinned Tiro, holding his nose.

\* \* \*

The two children crept through the passage until they came to a door. Tiro opened it and they stepped out behind a shrine under a tree.

Chloe gasped. All around them, huge marble palaces were bathed in silvery moonlight. They were in the very home of the gods.

## Chapter 8

# The Garden of Heavenly Scents

Chloe and Tiro made their way towards the largest temple, keeping to the shadows. Behind it, just as the giant had promised, was a walled garden. Its metal gate had a golden handle. Chloe glimpsed a carpet of white flowers. At its centre was a small patch of yellow ones.

"They must be the magic flowers," said Chloe.

The air was heavy with perfume. No wonder the giant had called it the Garden of Heavenly Scents.

Tiro turned the handle and they slipped in. "We'll fill our pockets with magic flowers," whispered Chloe.

* * *

The sun was starting to rise by the time they finished. They were almost ready to go, when–

"You! What are you two doing in there?"

A strange figure with a spear had appeared at the gate. It was half horse, half man. A centaur! He charged towards them.

"We're trapped," gasped Tiro. "What are we going to do?"

Chloe looked about her. What *could* they do? It looked as if their mission was going to fail at the last minute.

Then, suddenly, she heard the loud flapping of wings. It was Neb, swooping down from the sky. He landed softly in the garden and neighed loudly at the centaur, who backed off in fright.

Chloe and Tiro clambered onto Neb's back, making sure not to touch his injured wing. The last thing they saw of the mountain was a herd of centaurs galloping towards the garden. Then they were flying back to Axos.

But a shock was to greet them when they arrived home....

# Chapter 9

# Theseus

It was dark by the time Neb, Chloe and Tiro landed behind the palace stables. Chloe could hear shouting. People were running around frantically.

Two figures came striding to the stables, arguing loudly.

"I WON'T let you destroy my son, Theseus."

Chloe and Tiro ducked behind a bale of straw. The person shouting was the king.

"Your son is a dangerous monster," answered Theseus calmly. "That's why someone from this palace sent a pigeon carrying a message to me. They want him dead and they have paid me to kill him."

Chloe stifled a gasp. Now she realized why her uncle had stopped people leaving Axos. It was to prevent anyone fetching Theseus.

Theseus climbed on to his horse. "The monster might have got away from the dungeons," he chuckled, "but I shall hunt him down."

"So the minotaur has escaped," whispered Chloe as Theseus and the king were leaving. "We have to find him before Theseus does."

"I think I know where he might be," said Tiro.

They hurried back to Neb, and a few moments later they were up in the air again. Below them, they could see Theseus and his men riding away from the palace.

"Where are we going?" Chloe asked her friend.

"To a ruined temple in the Valley of Shadows," replied Tiro. "It was destroyed by an earthquake a long time ago. People believe it's cursed so no one will set foot in it – a perfect hiding place for the minotaur."

# *Chapter 10*

# The Cursed Temple

They flew on until they came to a deep valley. A brilliant moon appeared from behind the clouds and Chloe could just make out the ruined temple far below. Clambering over its broken columns was the minotaur. It spotted Neb, roared angrily and shook a fist at them.

Chloe landed Neb behind a tumbledown wall. Then she took the magic flowers out of her pockets and held them in her hands. Tiro added his.

Slowly, Chloe stepped into the temple.

The minotaur grunted and stomped towards her. Up close he was terrifying. His eyes were a fiery red, like burning coals. The tips on his horns looked sharp as spears.

"You fools!" he growled. "Don't you know what I am? Flee, while you still can."

Chloe's hands trembled as she held out the flowers. "Alexander… listen to me. I am your cousin, Chloe! Eat these. The nectar will cure you."

The minotaur glared at Chloe with a puzzled look. Then he reached out for the flowers.

"Aaarrgh!"

Suddenly a figure leapt out from behind a broken statue. A sword flashed in the moonlight! It was Theseus! He charged at the minotaur and knocked the flowers out of his hand.

"No!" Chloe screamed as Theseus and the minotaur started fighting. She scrambled on the ground looking for the flowers. But she couldn't see a single one. They had scattered on the night breeze.

Chloe looked at Tiro, a tear in her eye. She would never save her cousin now.

"Your highness!" her friend was holding out a flower. "There was one left in my pocket."

Chloe grabbed it and raced towards the minotaur.

"Here!"

The monster leapt towards her. He lashed out his tongue, licking up the flower. Then something very strange happened. A golden light shone all around him.

Slowly, the horns and bull's head melted away. They were replaced by Prince Alexander's face. The prince opened his eyes as if he were waking from a deep, deep sleep. The golden light around him dimmed.

Chloe ran forward and hugged Alexander tight. Then she turned to Theseus.

But he and his men were gone. Chloe heard their horses galloping away.

"You two have saved my life," said Alexander. "Thank you."

"We must get back to the palace and let your parents know you are safe," urged Chloe. "They are worried sick about you."

"Yes," agreed Prince Alexander. "But how will we get there?"

He gasped when he saw the winged horse, then quickly climbed on to his back behind Chloe and Tiro.

"Now we can start enjoying the summer," he said excitedly. "Who knows what other adventures we might have?"

## THE END

# FICTION EXPRESS

## THE READERS TAKE CONTROL!

**Have you ever wanted to change the course of a plot, change a character's destiny, tell an author what to write next?**

**Well, now you can!**

'My Cousin the Minotaur' was originally written for the award-winning interactive e-book website Fiction Express.

Fiction Express e-books are published in gripping weekly episodes. At the end of each episode, readers are given voting options to decide where the plot goes next. They vote online and the winning vote is then conveyed to the author who writes the next episode, in real time, according to the readers' most popular choice.

**www.fictionexpress.co.uk**

**WINNER**
Education Resources
Award for Innovation

# FICTION EXPRESS

## TALK TO THE AUTHORS

The Fiction Express website features a blog where readers can interact with the authors while they are writing. An exciting and unique opportunity!

## FANTASTIC TEACHER RESOURCES

Each weekly Fiction Express episode comes with a PDF of teacher resources packed with ideas to extend the text.

**"The teaching resources are fab and easily fill a whole week of literacy lessons!"**
Rachel Humphries, teacher at Westacre Middle School

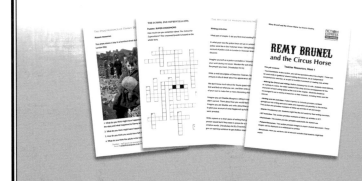

# FICTION EXPRESS

## Deena's Dreadful Day
### by Simon Cheshire

Deena is preparing for her big moment – a part in the local talent contest – but everything is going wrong. Her mum and dad are no help, and only her dog, Bert, seems to understand.

Will Deena and Bert make it to the theatre in time? Will her magic tricks work or will her dreadful day end in disaster?

ISBN 978-1-78322-569-9

# FICTI🗩N EXPRESS

## Ambush! A Robin Hood Adventure
### by Jan Burchett & Sara Vogler

Sam and Kate are servants in Nottingham Castle.
One day they overhear the Sheriff of Nottingham's
evil plan to ambush Robin Hood. They must warn the
outlaw! But how can they sneak out of the castle?
Will they even be able to find Robin in the dark and
mysterious Sherwood Forest? And will they reach him
before the sheriff and his men?

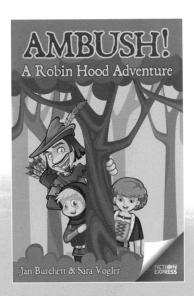

ISBN 978-1-78322-599-6

## Emery the Explorer: A Jungle Adventure
### by Louise John

When the postman delivers half of a mysterious treasure map through Emery's letterbox, the young explorer knows that a new adventure is about to begin. The trail leads him and his pet monkey, Spider, deep into the steamy Amazon jungle.

Can Emery survive the dangers of the rain forest? Will he succeed in finding the treasure before Dex D Saster, his biggest rival, or will his jungle adventure end in failure?

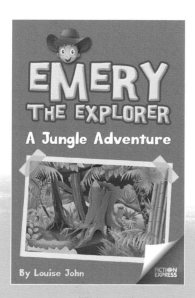

ISBN 978-1-78322-570-5

# FICTI●N EXPRESS

## Captain Jellybeard and the Giant South Sea Prawn
### by Simon Cheshire

Captain Jessica Jellybeard and her crew of pirates sail the high seas. When they read that there is a fortune to be made by capturing the legendary Giant South Sea Prawn, the race is on. But will Captain Jellybeard be first to the prize or will it be her enemy, the evil Captain Skullbone?

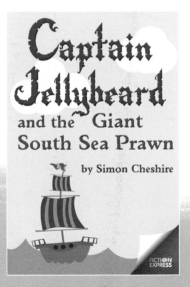

ISBN 978-1-78322-596-5

# FICTI●N EXPRESS

## The House on Strange Street
### by Simon Cheshire

Dad wants to buy the rundown house on Strange Street, but Joel and Zoe aren't so sure. The garden is overgrown, the paint is flaking off the windows and the roof leaks. Inside, the place is very dusty, creepy and spooky. It's full of weird noises and creaking floorboards, and... what was that? A shadow? Or was it some kind of scary creature?

Should the family risk it, and buy the house or get out of there as fast as they can?

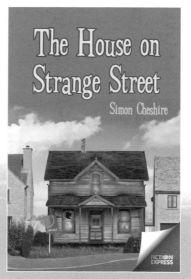

ISBN 978-1-78322-580-4

# FICTI🗨N EXPRESS

## The Sand Witch
by Tommy Donbavand

When twins Chris and Ella are left to look after
their younger brother on a deserted beach, they
expect everything to be normal, boring in fact. But
then something extraordinary happens! Will the
Sand Witch succeed in passing on her sandy curse
in this exciting adventure?

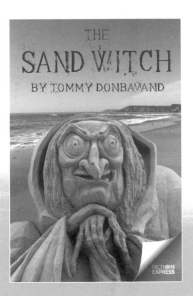

ISBN 978-1-78322-544-6

# FICTI●N EXPRESS

## Snaffles the Cat Burglar
### by Cavan Scott

When notorious feline felon Snaffles and his dim canine sidekick Bonehead are caught red-pawed trying to steal the Sensational Salmon of Sumatra, not everything is what it seems. Their capture leads them on a top-secret mission for the Ministry of Secret Shenanigans.

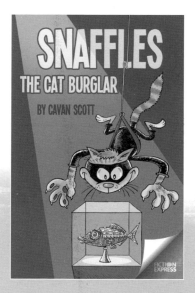

ISBN 978-1-78322-543-9

## About the Author

Saviour Pirotta is the best-selling author of many books for children. Originally from the sunny island of Malta he moved to England in his early twenties and worked as a storyteller before writing his first book.

As a child he was an avid reader and would read the lists of ingredients on food packets if he had nothing else to read. His favourite authors were C. S. Lewis and Enid Blyton. He also liked pirate stories like *Treasure Island* and *Peter Pan*.

Today he is a British citizen and lives in Saltaire, a world heritage site in West Yorkshire. His books include *The Orchard Book Of First Greek Myths* and *Firebird*, published by Templar. An expert on ancient Greek mythology and culture, Saviour loves travelling, especially to Greek islands. He enjoys cooking Mediterranean food, snorkelling, collecting old pictures and china and reading ghost stories in haunted places. He sleeps with the lights on.